W9-BRS-636

DOWN
to the SEA *in*
SHIPS

Philemon Sturges

illustrated by

Giles Laroche

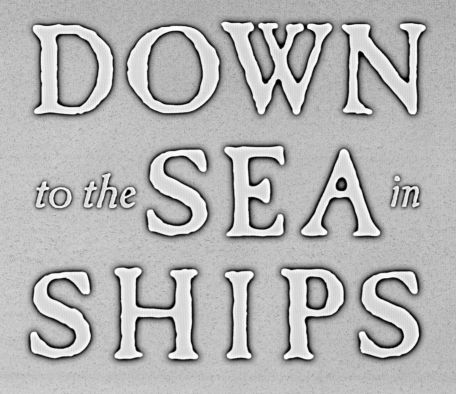

G. P. PUTNAM'S SONS

NEW YORK

To John, who cannot see,

but loves to sail—

at times with me!

—P. S.

To those who lost their lives

in the Grand Banks storm

of 1846.

—G. L.

With thanks to the collections at
Mystic Seaport, Mystic, Connecticut.

The ship on the jacket is an "East Indiaman" used in trade with the Orient. Indiamen sailed in the seventeenth and eighteenth centuries (this one from a painting done in the 1740s) and were the trading vessel of choice until the clipper ships were built.

On the title page is a gaiassa, a Nile vessel that has two tall sails hoisted right to the masthead like early European lateen sails. It sails upstream and floats downstream. It was used to carry cargo.

G. P. PUTNAM'S SONS

A division of Penguin Young Readers Group

Published by The Penguin Group

Penguin Group (USA) Inc., 375 Hudson Street, New York, NY 10014, U.S.A.

Penguin Group (Canada), 10 Alcorn Avenue, Toronto, Ontario, Canada M4V 3B2 (a division of Pearson Penguin Canada Inc.).

Penguin Books Ltd, 80 Strand, London WC2R 0RL, England.

Penguin Ireland, 25 St. Stephen's Green, Dublin 2, Ireland (a division of Penguin Books Ltd.).

Penguin Books India Pvt Ltd, 11 Community Centre, Panchsheel Park, New Delhi - 110 017, India.

Penguin Group (NZ), Cnr Airborne and Rosedale Roads, Albany, Auckland 1310, New Zealand (a division of Pearson New Zealand Ltd).

Penguin Books (South Africa) (Pty) Ltd, 24 Sturdee Avenue, Rosebank, Johannesburg 2196, South Africa.

Penguin Books Ltd, Registered Offices: 80 Strand, London WC2R 0RL, England.

 Published simultaneously in Canada. Manufactured in China by South China Printing Co. Ltd. Design by Cecilia Yung and Gina DiMassi. Text set in 12-point Columbus. The three-dimensional illustrations were created on a variety of paper surfaces through a combination of drawing, painting, and paper-cutting. Library of Congress Cataloging-in-Publication Data Sturges, Philemon. Down to the sea in ships / Philemon Sturges ; illustrated by Giles Laroche. p. cm. Summary: Poems describe a variety of watercraft, from birch bark canoes to cruise ships, and reveal their impact on the world. 1. Ships—Juvenile poetry. 2. Children's poetry, American. 3. Sea poetry, American. [1. Boats and boating—Poetry. 2. American poetry. 3. Sea poetry.] I. Laroche, Giles, ill. II. Title. PS3569.T877 D69 2005 [E]—dc21 2002067957

ISBN 0-399-23464-0

1 3 5 7 9 10 8 6 4 2

First Impression

The Beginning of Boat

Put a thing in a pail filled with water,

The water will overflow.

If the thing weighs more than the water that spills,

To the bottom that thing will go.

If lighter, the thing will bob and float

And so you have the beginning of boat.

A Birch Bark Canoe

If you wish to see the sea,

Build a sturdy boat like me

That's light and strong.

Then come along,

Follow river's winding way,

Watch herons stalk and beavers play.

Run the rapids, and then haul

Me round the waterfall.

And when, at last, the sea greets you,

Be grateful for your birch canoe.

A Viking Drakar

When people thought the world was flat,
In a land both cruel and cold
Some brazen men decided that
Earth's edge they must behold.
They sailed beside the ice and land
Into the sunset's glow . . .
But usually that hearty band
Would row.

For days they'd row and row and bail,
But if a fair wind blew,
They'd set their giant square red sail
And westward their ship flew.
For countless moons, that grizzled crew
Braved sleet and freezing gale.
Where they'd end, they never knew.
But we've found that lonely vale,
It's true—

That hearty Viking band found
Newfoundland!

Magellan

The *Santiago, Trinidad, Concepción, Victoria* and *San Antonio*

The north of the new land was frozen in ice.

How could the Spaniards get tea, silk, and spice?

Go south! There should be a way around.

A pass to the Eastern Sea must be found.

So five ships, with two-hundred-plus crew,

Joined Ferdinand Magellan. He knew what to do.

Follow the coast, check each river and bay.

Sail south, sail south, there must be a way!

The water grew cold, the weather turned foul,

The fierce roaring forties started to howl.

One ship rebelled. Its captain was bound,

And his ship, with all hands, was run aground.

They sailed far south near the endless day

Before they came to a watery way.

They found the passage, that they knew,

'Cause the water was salt and the tide ripped through.

As they ventured in, the williwaw blew.

It spun down from the mountain and frightened the crew.

One ship turned tail to her boundless shame,

But Magellan sailed on to misfortune and fame.

(continued)

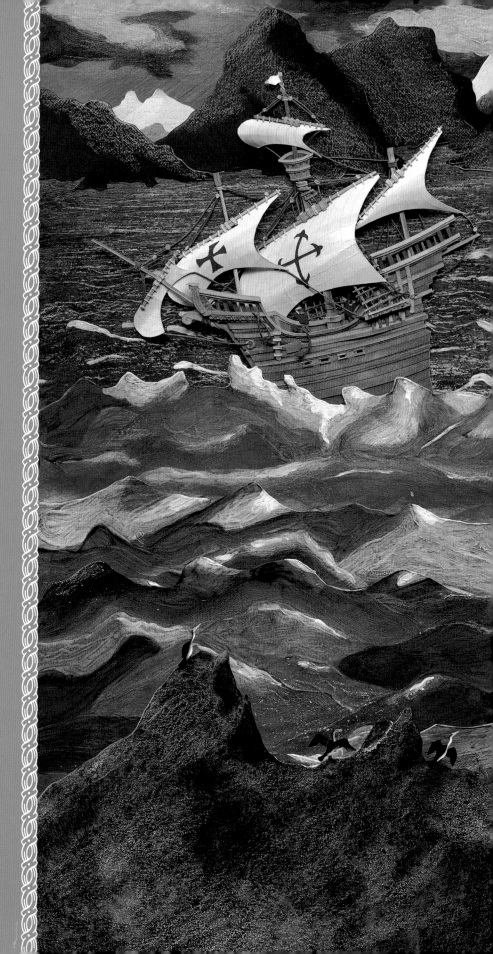

Three ships made it through. The new ocean was vast.

Their food and their water failed to last.

They ate leather and weevils, and captured some rain.

He and his crew went almost insane.

At last he found land. Soon after, he died

With a native's sharp lance thrust deep in his side.

His ships sailed on, but one was sunk.

Another was rotting. It soon became junk.

After thirty-six moons, just eighteen men

In their tiny ship came home again.

Whaling

Near the polar circles
Where there's no summer night
Is where the boldest whalers sailed
To glean whale oil for light.
That is where huge icebergs ride the swells.
That is where the mighty right whale dwells.
The whale's sweet oil lit the night
So Thomas Jefferson could write.

"Heave hearty, lads, for thar she blows,"
The Yankee steersman yelled.
The harpooner threw his sharp barbed spear;
Another whale was felled.
It slapped its fluke and sounded as it tried
To drag their six-man boat beneath the tide.
The whale's clear oil lit the night
So Thomas Jefferson could write.

The whale was towed beside the ship.
Its blubber, slick and cold,
Was peeled, then chunked and slowly boiled
Till oil filled the hold.
"All hands," the captain hollered, "yo-ho, yo-ho,
The ship is full! Hoist sail and home we'll go!"
The whale's pure oil lit the night
So Thomas Jefferson could write.

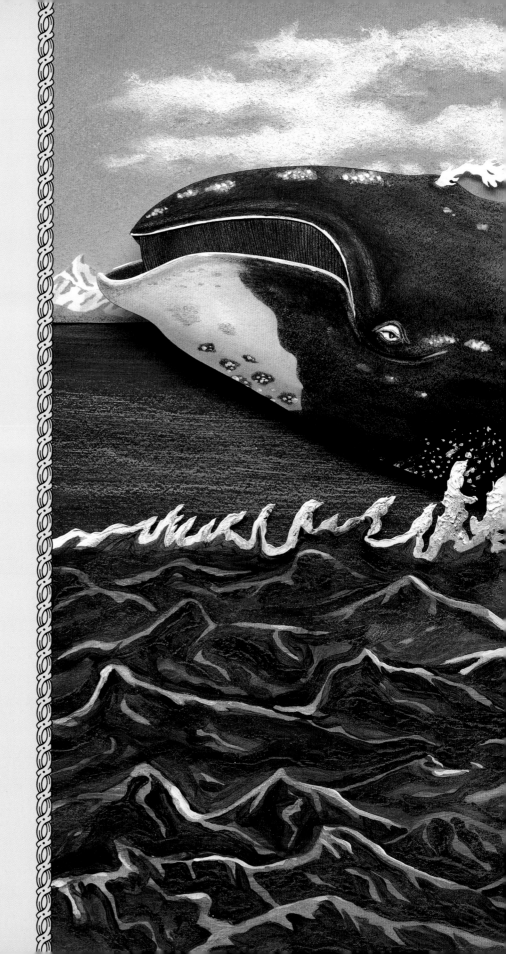

Catboat

When wind's behind, you run, your boat will zip.

When from the side, you reach, take care—

Your boat will tip!

But when wind you face!

Alas, alack,

You have to tack—

Go left, go right,

And then go back.

The seas you'll fight,

With all your might.

Takes twice as long to reach your place,

But tack too much, you'll lose the race.

So don't race, just sail, relax, have fun.

Feel cooling sea and warming sun.

Watch minnows leap and sleek terns dive

Where mackerel feed and fat seals thrive.

Go where ere the wind doth blow.

Follow time and tide's unending flow.

Then you'll return from way out there

Free of worry, fret, and care.

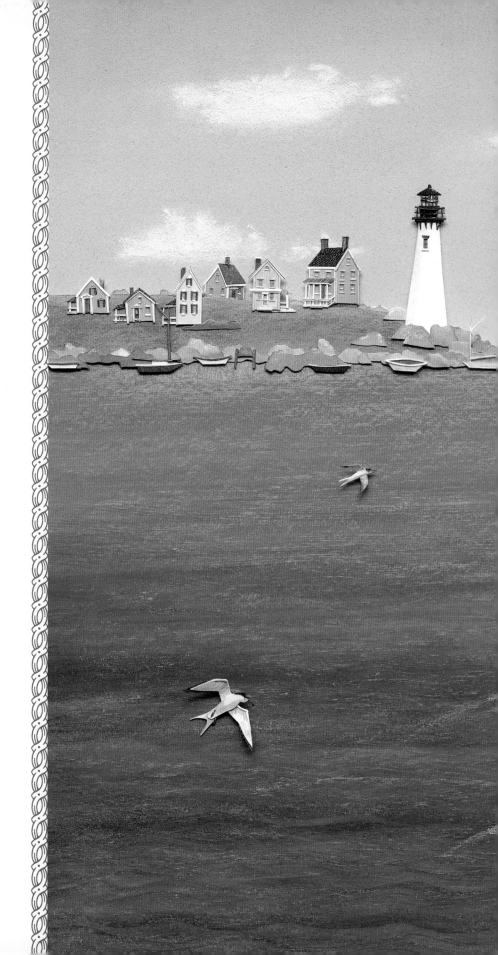

The Savannah

Savannah never had to tack,

She was a sailor's dream.

When wind was aft she forward flew;

When forward, she used steam!

When ill wind blew, her able crew

Set wheels on either side.

Steam hissed and sung, her great wheels spun,

Into the wind she'd glide.

Savannah steamed to England,

To Russia she did roam.

She was the first ship using steam

To cross and then come home.

The Flying Cloud

An incredible ship for an ocean trip
Was the clipper *Flying Cloud.*
Her towering spars could touch the stars—
She reached with her masts unbowed.
The man at the wheel could only feel
Disdain for the hurricane-cane-cane,
For it always appeared when the storm had cleared.
She'd rounded the Horn again.

So blow, ye winds, heigh-ho,
To 'Frisco we will go!
We'll stay no more on Yankee shore,
So set the skysails high-high-high.
We're off to celebrate
Inside the Golden Gate.
Our record stays—less'n ninety days
From New York—the *Cloud* can fly!

The Schooner

Not long ago in the shallow sea

On the shoals where the glacier used to be

Were cod.

By God, there were cod!

The old-timers said

You could walk on their backs

From the Cape to Marblehead!

There tall schooners set afloat

One lonely man each to a tiny boat.

With hooks and lines and buckets of bait

He'd sit in his dory and hardly wait—

A nibble, a bite, set the hook and haul.

A cod? A halibut? Big or small?

For year after year and day after day

The schooner's small dories fished away.

And, by God,

There were cod!

Then diesel trawling ships arrived

On those banks where the cod once thrived.

They dragged and hauled by night and day—

All living things were stripped away.

And now, dear God,

There are no cod!

The Mauretania

Her stacks spit soot, her turbines churn,

Her powerful propellers turn.

Sails are not needed.

Her coal-fed boilers (twenty-five)

Bring this leviathan alive.

The wind blows by, unheeded.

Her great horn blares, the fireboat sprays,

Mauretania, in just five days,

Has crossed the sea.

With torch held high, she greets the crowd.

Those joy-teared travelers gasp aloud

At Liberty.

For be they rich, or be they poor—

Some will fail, most will endure—

They're glad to be

In this new land where hope is found,

Where opportunities abound,

And men are free.

Tugboat

Tooot——tooot peep-peep peep-peep,

Go slow astern,

Toooot Toooot,

Your bow's clear. We'll push, you turn!

Tooot——tooot peep-peep,

Put on some way,

Tooot peep-peep,

You're free—have a nice day!

"Tooot——tooot peep-peep-peep-peep,

Good-bye!" the tugboat cries.

"Baarooooooooooom!

Grazie—thank you much!" the ship replies.

It churns its mighty engine, heads round the earth.

The husky tugboat turns, chugs to its berth.

Puget Sound

The sails are gone, most people go by air.

Huge steel ships take goods most everywhere—

Tankers from Alaska's frigid sound—

Giant redwood logs are westward bound.

From Korea: car-filled ships.

From Taiwan: computer chips.

Huge containers on their way

To Manila, Hong Kong, Perth, Bombay.

Yet men still face the wind's wild roar

To cross the sea to Singapore.

Beneath Mount Rainier's towering peak

Ferries ply as sailors seek

To share the patch of sunny sky they found

On Puget Sound.

The Cruise Ship

On this ship you go
Out to sea and never know
You're there.

There are swimming pools and color TVs,
Trampolines, clowns, fake coconut trees.
There are gyms, and playgrounds, and all kinds of stores.
There are libraries, movies, and dancing indoors
In fully conditioned air.

You set out to sea for a week or two,
Play hide-and-seek with the captain and crew,
Eat burgers and shrimp, Tex-Mex barbecue . . .
Do all that you've ever wanted to do
As you cruise away
To nowhere.

The Reliance

John Herreshoff loved to sail, though he was blind.

So little brother Nat watched for rocks as they would roam

In *Meteor* to Usher Cove and then back home.

John taught Nat to hold the tiller and feel

The water coursing round the graceful curving hull and keel

Of their small sloop.

Soon Nat learned to gently carve and sand

A model of the boat within his mind. His skillful hand

Would carefully smooth and shape the bow

So it could speed through water calm,

Or through chop plow.

(*Reliance* was the greatest of these craft—

Fifty yards from fore to aft—

Two hundred feet from water to her topmost spar,

'Bout twenty feet and five from rail to rail—

Sixteen thou' square feet of sail—

At twenty knots she'd beat a chugging motorcar!)

Though blind, John had amazing memory

And so he ran the company

That built the ships that formed within Nat's mind.

They made the fastest ships that ever sailed the sea.

Six times their swift yachts headed up.

They'd crossed the mark in victory

And claimed the Cup.

Adrift in Usher Cove

Be still.

Ignore the distant sounds of Man and thunder.

Look deep into the sea.

Be filled with wonder.